UNCLE LEO'S ADVENTURES in the Romanian Steppes

Yannets Levi has written books and for television. Born in Israel to a family of storytellers, he remembers being surrounded by stories ever since he was a kid, told by his parents, uncles and aunts.

His Uncle Leo's Adventures series is one of Israel's most popular children's book series and has sold more than 450,000 copies in Israel alone. The series has also been published in the Czech Republic, South Korea and Japan. He has also written another children's book, *Mrs Rosebud is No Monster*, and two books for adults.

Yaniv Shimony is a graduate of the Bezalel Academy of Art and Design in Jerusalem, considered the top art school in Israel. After completing his studies, he worked as Art Director in some of Israel's largest advertising agencies. Currently, his work focuses on illustrating children's books. In 2008, Shimony won an award for Children's Book Illustration from the Israel Museum for his work in *Uncle Leo's Adventures in the Romanian Steppes.*

Other Books in the Series:

Uncle Leo's Adventures in the Siberian Jungle

Uncle Leo's Adventures in the Swiss Desert

Unlce Leo's Adventures in the West Pole

UNCLE LEO'S ADVENTURES in the Romanian Steppes

Yannets Levi

Illustrated by Yaniv Shimony
Translated by Margo Eyon

RED TURTLE
RUPA

**For my nephews and nieces,
with whom the stories were born**

Published in Red Turtle by
Rupa Publications India Pvt. Ltd 2014
7/16, Ansari Road, Daryaganj
New Delhi 110002

Sales centres:
Allahabad Bengaluru Chennai
Hyderabad Jaipur Kathmandu
Kolkata Mumbai

First published in Hebrew in 2008

Translated by Margo Eyon

This edition published by arrangement with Asia Publishers Int.,
Israel (asia01@netvision.net.il) through Writer's Side, India

ISBN: 978-81-291-3463-9

First impression 2014

10 9 8 7 6 5 4 3 2 1

Contents

Introduction

You probably won't believe a word I say. You'll probably think I'm a liar. You might even laugh at me. But I swear that everything I'm about to tell you really happened. No lies. I didn't make up any of it. And if I am lying, then...then…my ears should fall off, because every last thing I'm going to tell you I heard with my own ears from my Uncle Leo.

Uncle Leo comes to visit us every Wednesday. Uncle Leo isn't like any ordinary uncle. My father once said, 'Uncle Leo isn't the kind of uncle you can just buy in any old store. He's more like a special-order kind of uncle.'

My big brother, on the other hand, doesn't believe anything Uncle Leo says. 'It's all a bunch of chopped baloney,' he always says, which is exactly like baloney, but my brother thinks that chopped baloney is much balonier than your regular sliced baloney. But what does my brother know? He thinks that stories are for children and that he's not a kid any more, but he *is*, even though he's older than I am.

So that's it. I'm going to tell you everything that Uncle Leo told me about the Romanian steppes. It's the whole truth and only the truth, even if my brother thinks otherwise.

Oh, and by the way, my name is Andy, my father's name is Eliot, my mother's is Daphne, my brother's is Graham, and my Uncle Leo's—as you might have guessed—is Uncle Leo.

How Uncle Leo Got Stuck on a Cloud

One Wednesday, Uncle Leo, Graham and I were sitting on the balcony. It was a wintry day and we were looking at the clouds in the sky. I kept seeing people and other shapes in the clouds: a tiger, a lizard, a man's face, spectacles. And each time the wind blew, it moved the clouds around and changed their shapes. It was fun, so I said, 'This is such fun! I wish I could ride on the clouds.'

'That's ridiculous,' said Graham. 'You can't ride a cloud. Clouds are made of water vapour.'

Uncle Leo gazed at the clouds and said, 'I rode a cloud once.'

'What? Really?' I asked.

'Yes, it happened to me,' replied Uncle Leo.

Graham said, 'I'm going to go play on the computer,' and left the balcony as if he hadn't even heard what Uncle Leo had just said. Uncle Leo's story didn't seem to interest him much.

'When did it happen? When did you ride a cloud?' I asked Uncle Leo.

'When I was in the Romanian steppes,' he answered. 'I didn't just ride a cloud; I got stuck on it.'

'No way! Can you really get stuck on a cloud?' I asked, shifting my glance from Uncle Leo's face to the clouds floating through the sky.

'It all began when I was hiking through a thick forest in the land of the giants on the Romanian steppes,' began Uncle Leo. 'I'd gone to the land of the giants to study how the giants live. Suddenly, I spied a small note pinned to a tree trunk with an arrow. I went over and saw something written on it, and this is what it said:

Far away on a mountain peak,
Be you so bold as to go and seek,
Prove your true measure
By climbing high, digging deep,
And a wondrous treasure
Will be yours to keep.

'On the other side of the note was a little map explaining how to reach the treasure. I decided to immediately go and find it. I followed the path until I arrived at the foot of a tall, tall mountain. How high was it? So high that I couldn't see its top. That mountain was so high that its top reached beyond the clouds!

'I started to climb the mountain. Unfortunately, no one had been on the path leading up the mountain for hundreds of years, so it was overgrown with weeds and thorns. I had to leap and skip so the thorns wouldn't prick my legs. I wanted to reach the treasure very badly.

'I kept climbing, using the weeds as ropes for support. With great difficulty, I managed to reach the top. By then, I was panting and sweating heavily, and shaking from head to toe. I could barely see anything. Just fog. The peak was completely covered by a huge cloud! It was very high up and chilly.

'Trembling with cold, I studied the map again and walked up to where the treasure was hidden. I dug into the earth with my bare hands, like a snooping dog, and finally pulled out an enormous chest. I opened the chest and found a shiny red stone inside! It was this big:

'It was a remarkable stone! It was a wondrous stone! Such a big stone! I had never seen a stone so beautiful! I stretched out my hand to take the stone out from the huge chest, but just at that moment, the wind started blowing. The wind blew off the cloud that covered the peak, and carried me along with it!

'The cloud sailed on, and I saw the mountaintop moving farther away. *Now how will I ever reach the red stone*, I thought to myself. I was so disappointed! But soon enough, I forgot all about the stone, because I looked around me and realized that I was stuck on a cloud.'

Uncle Leo fell silent and said no more.

I couldn't help asking, 'Then what did you do, Uncle Leo?'

'About what, Andy?' asked Uncle Leo.

'About the cloud!' I cried.

'What cloud?' Uncle Leo asked.

'The cloud you got stuck on. How did you get down?'

'Oh! *That* cloud!' said Uncle Leo. 'Yes, that was indeed a tough one. I didn't know what to do. I peeked down, and the land of the giants was far, far away. The giants down there looked as small as grains of sand, and the trees looked like blades of grass. I didn't know what to do. How could I get off the cloud? If I jumped, I'd smash into the ground and turn into a pancake!

'All of a sudden, I saw flying dots in the distance. I strained my eyes and made out that the flying dots were a flock of wild geese migrating to warmer lands.

'*They can get me down*, I thought to myself and began calling out, "Help, help! I'm stuck on a cloud! Help! Help! I'm stuck on a cloud!"

'My voice echoed through the sky, but the flock of

geese was too far away to hear me clearly. They didn't hear me calling for help. They didn't know that I was in trouble. I called again, "Help, help! I'm stuck on a cloud!"

'"What? What did he say, that man over there on the cloud?" the commander of the flock of geese asked his second-in-command.

'"I think he yelled, 'Clap, clap! I'm sticking around!'"

'I cried again with all my might, "Help, help! I'm stuck on a cloud!"

'But the wild geese heard, "Clap, clap! I'm sticking around!" And sure enough, they all clapped with their beaks and cheered for me, but they kept flying on their course to the warm lands. And I stayed stuck on the cloud.'

'So what did you do?' I asked Uncle Leo.

'I didn't know what to do,' he answered. 'The geese had gone, but a dandy crow came along. The crow came and sat down on the cloud. He pulled out a mirror from inside his feathers and studied his beak in the mirror. "Oh, what a magnificent beak I have! Oh, what gorgeous wings I have! Oh, I am so very handsome! *Que bellisimo!* I'm just in love with myself!" boasted the crow.

'"Oh, crow," I said, "I'm stuck on this cloud. Could you help me get down to earth?"

'"Hey, amigo, what are you talking about? Why don't you get down by yourself?"

'"How can I get down? I don't have wings. If I jump, I'll turn into a pancake!" I told him.

'"Mamma mia! This is not possible! What kind of a bird are you?" asked the crow.

'"I'm not a bird. I'm a human being."

'"Caw caw caw, caw caw caw," laughed the crow. "Amigo, you've really gotten yourself into a pickle. Everyone knows people can't fly!"

'"Exactly!" I said. "So could you kindly give me a ride back down to the land of the giants?"

'"You must be joking!" the crow cried out. "Santa Maria! What has the world come to! Do you have any idea how much work and tender loving care I put into these feathers? If you rode on my back you would rumple all my feathers! There's no way I'm taking you down!"

'Nothing helped. I tried to promise the crow I would sit gently on his back. I suggested I'd scrub his feathers when we land. I even proposed dry-cleaning them. Nothing would convince him. The crow flew off with a big laugh: "Caw caw caw, caw caw caw!"

'I didn't know what to do. I could no longer see the top of the mountain. The cloud had drifted away from it. The sun was starting to set, and it was getting dark. I couldn't see any other birds on the horizon, and the earth below looked farther away than ever. I thought, *I don't want the red stone any longer. I don't need any treasure. I just need to get off this cloud!*

'Suddenly in the distance I made out a large cloud coming nearer and nearer to the cloud I was sitting on. "Oh my!" I cried. "When the two clouds bump into each other, lightning will flash, thunder will roll, it will start to rain, the clouds will fall down to earth as raindrops, and I—I'll fall down to earth and turn into a pancake!"

'The clouds came closer and closer to each other, getting bigger and bigger, and then—ZIG and ZAG blazed a bolt of lightning! BOOM and BANG roared a bolt of thunder! And raging rain started to pour down. The more it rained, the smaller and smaller the cloud became, and I knew that in another second, the whole cloud would rain down to earth, and I would fall along with the raindrops. The last droplets of the cloud started to fall, and I tumbled down with them. I tried to hold on to them, but my hands only got wet. *That's it, then! I'm going to be a pancake*, I thought, while falling to earth.'

Uncle Leo sipped from his teacup and gazed up at the clouds with a nostalgic look.

'Uncle Leo, were you really squashed like a pancake?!' I asked.

'No, I didn't turn into a pancake because I didn't land on the ground,' Uncle Leo continued. 'I landed on something soft. I felt around to see if I was in one piece. I could only see cloth spread out around me, and under it, there was something soft and springy like Jell-O. *Where am I,* I wondered.

'Suddenly, I heard loud snoring. I followed the sound of the snoring until I reached the face of a giant woman. I wasn't that surprised, I *was* in the land of the giants, after all! "What great luck! I've landed on the belly of a giantess," I told myself.

'The giantess was sleeping and snoring. I woke her up carefully and said, "Thank you very much! You saved my life!"

'"Who are you?" wondered the giantess.

'"I'm Uncle Leo," I answered.

"'And how did you get on my tummy?"

"'From the sky," I said, pointing upward. "I fell from the clouds with the raindrops and landed on your stomach! You saved my life. It was a really soft landing!"

"'Oh my, was it indeed?" said the giantess. "You don't know how happy I am to hear that. I've always hated my fat stomach. I always thought it's too big. I was always ashamed of it. But now I know there's a use for it. It can save people who fall out of the sky!"

'I felt that words just weren't enough to thank the giantess. So I told her about the red stone: "Do you see that far mountain there on the horizon? The one whose peak reaches up to the clouds? On that peak is a treasure chest, and in the chest is a large, shiny red stone."

'The giantess thanked me and walked straight to the mountain. She was so tall that she didn't have to climb to the top. Her head reached the sky. She just poked among the clouds that covered the peak and pulled out

the stone. But the stone didn't impress her. Compared to the enormous giantess, the red stone was teensy. "What am I going to do with such a tiny rock?" she said, tossing it over her shoulder.

'The stone flew through the air and landed at my feet. To me, of course, the stone was very, very big. I picked it up and exclaimed, "I did it! I got the red stone after all!"

'And that's the end of the story,' said Uncle Leo. Uncle Leo and I were quiet for a while, gazing up at the clouds in the sky. The sun had already started to set and the clouds looked orange, red and even purple.

At dinner, I asked my brother Graham, 'Did you know that Uncle Leo really did get stuck on a cloud once?'

'Come on, what nonsense he tells you! You can't get stuck on clouds,' said my brother.

'Sure you can,' I said at once.

'Those are all tall tales,' said Graham.

'They're *not* tall tales; they're Uncle Leo tales,' I said.

'Same thing,' said Graham. 'Why do you insist on believing everything Uncle Leo tells you?'

'Why not believe Uncle Leo?' said Mom. 'Uncle Leo told me many wonderful stories when I was young. I wish I still had the time to sit and listen to his stories today.'

'Yes, but they're just stories,' repeated Graham.

'So what?' said Mom.

Dad came into the kitchen.

'Tell me, did you water the plants?' Mom asked him.

'Uh, no,' said Dad, 'I didn't have time. I had to get something ready for work tomorrow.'

'It's the same old story every day,' said Mom. 'You and your nonsensical stories.'

'You see?' my brother whispered to me, 'Stories are nonsense.'

'But Uncle Leo's stories are different,' I whispered back to him.

That night, I lay in bed and closed my eyes. I fell asleep and dreamt that I was on a cloud with Uncle Leo, flying over the land of the giants in the Romanian steppes.

Why Uncle Leo Loves His Four Hairs

When Mom announced on Wednesday that it was about time that I had my hair cut, I immediately told her, 'I don't want to!'

Graham, sitting on the couch next to me, said, 'You're all curls. What are you, a poodle?'

'I don't want a haircut,' I said, and then Uncle Leo came in. Uncle Leo has only four hairs on his head, and he just loves them. Sometimes he dyes them yellow, and sometimes purple.

'The boy doesn't want a haircut,' said Mom. She meant me, because that's what she calls me when she's complaining.

'I don't like getting my hair cut either,' said Uncle Leo, winking at me.

But Mom told him, 'How could you get your hair cut anyway, Uncle Leo? You're bald!'

'Bald! How am I bald?' Uncle Leo seemed hurt. 'I'm not bald. I have four hairs on my head. You call that bald?'

'Four hairs is not hair! That's bald!' Mom replied.

'Not when you have hair like mine. These four hairs once saved my life!'

'Really?' I asked.

'Well, I have to run to work. We'll deal with your haircut tomorrow,' Mom said as she left the house.

Graham stayed in the living room to watch television. Uncle Leo and I sat in the balcony.

'How did your four hairs save your life?' I asked Uncle Leo.

'It happened when I was working in a travelling circus in the Romanian steppes,' replied Uncle Leo.

'You used to work in a circus?' I asked.

'Oh, yes. And I had a special job. They had a cannon in the circus. At the end of each show, I would crawl into the barrel of the cannon and they would shoot me from one end of the circus tent to the other, where I would land in a safety net.'

'And what does that have to do with your four hairs?' I asked.

'It has everything to do with them,' said Uncle Leo. 'The cannon was operated by this dwarf named Chapek. Every day, he would put gunpowder in the cannon. At the end of the show, Chapek would ignite the gunpowder at the right moment, and the cannon would shoot me into the safety net.

'But Chapek liked to drink wine, and once, when he drank too much, he forgot that he had already put gunpowder in the cannon, and he put in another load. So the cannon had double the amount of gunpowder, and when Chapek lit it at the end of the show, the cannon shot me so hard and so far that I ripped a hole in the ceiling of the circus tent and went flying way beyond it.

I flew through the air until I reached a forest. I landed in a tree, and my hairs wrapped themselves around one of its branches. I hung there by my hairs and that's what kept me from falling. I'll never forget that my four hairs saved my life!

'The circus manager called a rescue squad. They brought a long, long, long ladder, rested it against the tree, and climbed up to me. The commander of the rescue squad came at me holding scissors in his hand.

'"What are you going to do?" I asked him.

'"I'm going to cut your hair with these scissors to free you from the branch."

'"Absolutely not!" I cried. "No one touches these hairs. I love them. They saved my life. Don't touch my hairs with those scissors."

'The commander of the rescue squad climbed down the ladder, and the rescue squad returned to the station.'

'And what did you do?' I asked Uncle Leo. 'How did you get down from the tree?'

'I waited,' answered Uncle Leo.

'Waited for what?' I asked.

'I waited for my hairs to grow. Spring passed, and then summer came, and my hairs got longer and longer.

After summer came autumn. The longer my hair grew, the closer I got to the ground. I waited until I reached the ground. It happened during the second or third winter. After reaching the ground, I climbed back up to the branch and untangled the knot of hair,' said Uncle Leo, adding a moment later: 'So how can anyone say I'm bald, when I have four such wonderful hairs on my head?'

At dinner, I told Mom, Dad and Graham what Uncle Leo had told me, how his four hairs had saved his life when he was working in a circus on the Romanian steppes. I ended by saying, 'So he's not, in fact, bald. He has four hairs on his head that saved him!'

'Four hairs on a head is a bald head,' said Graham.

I looked at Mom. 'It's true. Four hairs aren't enough to be not bald,' said Mom. 'Even Dad is bald, and he has a lot more than four hairs.'

'What's that supposed to mean?' Dad complained. 'You think I'm bald? I might have less hair than I used to, but you still can't call me bald,' he said, feeling around with his hand to check that he still had hair on his head.

'But Uncle Leo's hairs saved his life! Being bald never did anything good for him,' I said.

Mom looked at Dad, and Dad gave Mom the look he has when he is offended, even if he doesn't admit it.

'Okay, maybe you're right. It's better to see the glass as half full,' Mom finally said, laying her hand on Dad's hair.

'So I don't have to get a haircut?' I asked. 'Hair can save lives.'

'Of course you need to get your hair cut,' said Mom. 'You have too much hair on your head, and we're not sending you to work in a circus.'

How Uncle Leo Turned into a Cockroach

Once, when Uncle Leo and I were sitting in the balcony, a cockroach crossed the floor in front of us. I was so scared of that cockroach! I immediately jumped up on the chair and yelled, 'Roach, roach!' I hoped the cockroach would just go on his way without touching me.

'What's wrong?' asked Uncle Leo.

'Ew! Yuck! There's a roach over there!' I said, pointing at the cockroach.

'Wait a second! Why *yuck*? What are you afraid of? I know that cockroach.'

'What? You know it?' I asked.

'Sure do,' Uncle Leo said and started talking to the roach. 'Hey there, long time no see. How are you doing? Where've you been?'

The cockroach was silent. It stood in place, moving its feelers. It seemed to be looking straight into Uncle Leo's eyes.

'You don't say!' said Uncle Leo, and then he began to talk to the cockroach in a language I couldn't understand. I think it was the language they speak on the Romanian steppes.

'You aren't going to believe this, Andy, but he just arrived in our country a couple of weeks ago on a migrants' ship,' Uncle Leo translated the roach's antennae language for me. 'He and two friends of his sang "Travelin' Man" the whole way here, but he didn't think it was going to be so rainy.'

The cockroach went on his way, and Uncle Leo sat back down in the armchair.

I sat down as well.

'Ah, there's nothing like being a cockroach,' sighed Uncle Leo.

'Really?' I asked.

'I know it from personal experience, since I was once

a cockroach,' said Uncle Leo.

'Honest? You were once a cockroach?' I was amazed.

'Yes. It happened when I was on the Romanian steppes and got into an argument with this sorcerer. I told him there's no such thing as sorcerers in the real world; they only exist in legends. He was so insulted that he put a curse on me, turning me into a roach for a year. He uttered a short spell and then left.

'At first I didn't notice anything different, but when I went to the mirror and saw my reflection, I understood I really *had* turned into a roach! I got quite a fright! First, I realized that the sorcerer was right—there is such a thing as sorcerers, and they can even turn people into cockroaches. Second, I was sorry to be a cockroach and I wanted very badly to turn human again, but the sorcerer had vanished and I couldn't even beg him to give me my human body back.'

'What did you do?'

'I wanted to cry. I tried to cry but I couldn't. Roaches don't have tears. I only managed to move my feelers. But quite soon I discovered that roaches have a lot of advantages in life, and I was even happy to be a roach.'

'Really? What kind of advantages?' I asked.

'First off, you don't have to pay taxes. Plus, I could get on buses, ships and planes without buying a ticket. I could also fly with my own wings. I could get into all sorts of small places that human beings will never even know about. I could go through locked doors—just by going through the crack between the door and the floor. And another thing—I wasn't disgusted by the smell of sewage. On the contrary, the stench was like perfume to me, like the sweet smell of flowers. It was wonderful,' said Uncle Leo, his eyes staring forward, as if seeing something that wasn't there.

'It wasn't long before I started enjoying my life as a cockroach. Every evening I'd go to a roach party in a different sewer. What a wild time we had at those parties! Dancing, singing, telling stories, talking about roach politics—just fabulous! At one party I even met a lady-roach. Our feelers intertwined, and it was love at first touch. We used to go everywhere together. She was great. After a while, we had roach babies.

'We had ten children, and these were their names:

Greenroach, the gardener

Roachima, who could predict the future

Roachelina, the beautiful ballerina

Roacharoni, who loved macaroni

Roacholowski, who wore glasses

Roacholate, who was crazy about Hershey's Kisses

Roachamba, who loved to dance the samba

Roachsqueak, who was just a little guy

Roacheetah, who was like a jungle animal

And last but not least, Simon—named after my roach wife's father.

'We lived happily. We didn't have to work. The sewer was at our disposal in every house and at every street corner. Life was beautiful and every single one of our children was a success story.

'But there were also some things that we hated:

We hated shoes, because they were always being thrown at us.

We hated rain, because it's really hard to sing when your feelers are wet.

We hated cats, because they liked to torture us.

But people, we actually liked. We knew that without people we wouldn't have much food, garbage or sewage.

'One day, my roach wife asked me, "Why are people afraid of us? After all, we like them."

"'They're afraid of us because they think we're dirty," I explained.

"'Me? Me dirty? How ridiculous!" cried my wife. "I clean my feelers every day with fresh sewage water! And I shower every week in the local sewer pool! Cleanliness and hygiene are the most important things to us. What nerve! What an insult! Cockroaches have feelings too!"

'My roach wife was very offended. I didn't know what to tell her. I went to her and stroked her feelers.

'Time went by. Each day was more wonderful than the last. I completely forgot what it was like to be human. I even forgot that the sorcerer had turned me into a cockroach. But at the end of a year, the sorcerer returned.

"'I've come to turn you back into a human being!" he announced.

"'What? What are you talking about?" I cried. "I don't want to be a human being. I like being a roach. This isn't a curse at all; it's a blessing! I have a dear wife. I have ten lovely children. I enjoy life. I can fly, go through closed doors, sneak in anywhere, and I don't even have to pay taxes."

'"A curse is a curse, and its end can't be undone," said the sorcerer. "I must turn you back into a human."

'"Just wait a minute!" I shouted. "At least let me say goodbye to my family!"

'I went to each of my children and said farewell. I gave each one of them a tip for life:

'"Greenroach, remember to fertilize the plants."

'"Roachima, please predict a nice brown future for us."

'"Roachelina, character counts too, not just looks."

'"Roacharoni, I hope you go to Italy someday like you've dreamed of."

'"Roacholowski, don't let it get to you if someone calls you four-eyes."

'"Roacholate, be sure to brush after eating chocolate."

'"Roachamba, always keep the rhythm!"

'"Roachsqueak, know that your strength lies in your smallness."

'"Roacheetah, control that wild beast inside you."

'"Simon, here, take a penny for the pieman."

'Then, with quivering feelers I approached my roach wife. Our feelers wrapped around each other. "Farewell, my love. I'll never forget you," I told her. I faced the entire family and said, "You're staying here in the sewer and I'm going to live in a house like people do. But don't worry, I'll drop by now and again to visit. We'll still see each other."

'And then the sorcerer came right up to me, spat out a few magic words, and I became human again.'

Uncle Leo was silent, adding after a moment, 'Cockroaches have feelings too.'

The story was so sad that I felt a lump in my throat. I completely forgot that I was afraid of roaches.

'And how did it feel, being human again?' I asked.

'Humans have some advantages, too. For instance, I get to tell you about my adventures on the Romanian steppes,' said Uncle Leo. 'That's fun.'

That evening I sat in the living room with Mom, Dad and Graham. As we watched television, a cockroach

passed by on the carpet.

'Hey, there's a roach!' said Graham.

'Where, where?' asked Dad. He was so frightened that he leaped right up on the couch. 'Oh no! A cockroach! It really is a cockroach!' he called out, pointing at the roach.

Graham went over and tried to step on the roach.

The roach looked just like the one Uncle Leo and I had met. So I cried, 'No, Graham! Get away from him!'

'What, are you afraid of it?' asked Graham.

'No,' I replied. 'That roach is a friend of Uncle Leo's!'

'What?!' cried Mom and Graham in unison.

'A friend of Uncle Leo's?' asked Dad.

'Yes,' I said.

'Who told you that?' Mom asked.

'Uncle Leo,' said I.

'He's making things up again,' said Graham.

'Cockroaches don't hate us, Dad,' I explained to him. 'You don't have to be scared of them.'

'Scared? I'm not scared,' said Dad, forcing himself to sit back down on the couch. After a moment he said, 'Okay, maybe you're right.'

The cockroach had escaped in the meantime. He probably went off to some party in our sewage pipes.

Graham sat back down on the couch as well.

'Cockroaches have feelings too,' I said.

'What nonsense!' said Graham.

'Why *wouldn't* they have feelings?' I asked.

'Actually, you might be right,' said Mom. 'Who knows?'

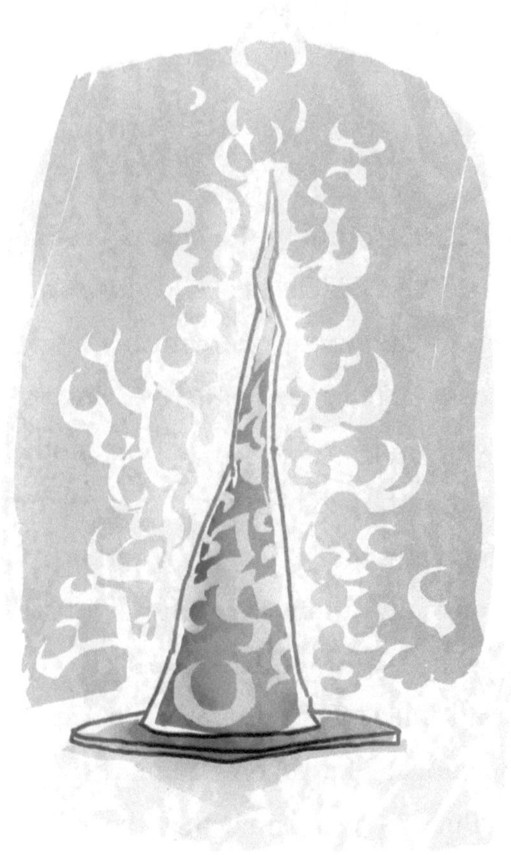

Uncle Leo, Court Jester in the Upsidown Kingdom

Once I was sitting in the balcony eating rice with Uncle Leo. Uncle Leo laid down his fork and started eating the rice with his fingers.

'Uncle Leo, you're eating with your fingers!' I said.

'That's right,' said Uncle Leo, putting another handful of rice in his mouth. I remembered that my mother told me that eating with your fingers is a barbaric habit. And my mother only says that something is a barbaric habit if she really and truly doesn't like it.

'Andy,' said Uncle Leo, 'there are places where you eat with your fingers, and there are places where you eat with sticks. But did you know that the mothers in the walk-on-your-hands kingdom tell their children, "Don't eat with your toes!"'

'Why do they say, "Don't eat with your toes," and not "Don't eat with your fingers"?' I asked.

'Because in the walk-on-your-hands kingdom, everyone walks on their hands and holds their knife and fork with their toes.'

'How do they sit down?' I asked.

'With their heads down and their legs leaning against the back of the chair,' answered Uncle Leo.

'Where is this kingdom?' I asked.

'The walk-on-your-hands kingdom is in a faraway, unknown province in the Romanian steppes. I visited there once,' said Uncle Leo, his mouth full of rice. After swallowing, he went on: 'Once, on one of my journeys to the Romanian steppes, I reached the gate of a city surrounded by a wall. Everything seemed to be normal there: a high wall with a few turrets, but one thing was upside down—the guard at the gate. He wore armor and weapons like any regular guard, but he wasn't standing on his feet. He was standing on his hands.

'"Hello," I said to him.

'"Who are you? What are you?" yelped the guard,

eyeing me suspiciously.

'"I'm Uncle Leo, and I'm a human being."

'"Why are you such a sight? Why don't you stand up right?" asked the guard, and I asked him, "Why are *you* such a sight?"

'"Why are you upside down?" asked the guard, and I asked him, "Why are *you* upside down?"

'The upside-down guard didn't know what to say and sank into thought for a moment. He shifted his weight from hand to hand and finally said, "I shall take you to our honourable king. He's never seen such a wonderful thing."

'"So this is a kingdom," said I. "And what is this kingdom called?"

'"You have come to the Kingdom of Upsidown. Welcome, and do take a look around."

'The guard opened the gate, instructing, "Follow me."

'I marched behind him, as a strange kingdom unfolded before me: all the men, all the women, and all the children—everyone walked on their hands. Everyone was—upside down! I passed through the kingdom's streets and marketplace. All the people stopped and gave me upside-down, amazed looks. I heard them whispering,

"Who is that? What is that? How is it walking? This is so shocking!" One boy even asked his mother loudly, "Mommy, why is that man walking on his feet?" And his mother immediately shushed him, "Raising your voice isn't polite, my sweet."

'I saw all kinds of strange things in the Kingdom of Upsidown:

The windows in the houses were close to the ground so that people's heads could look out of them.

Upside-down people carried boxes in their feet. When people smiled, it looked like their mouths were sad.

When people got upset, they waved their feet around in the air.

'I kept walking behind the guard, feeling like an alien from another planet. We reached the strange palace. We went up the stairs and through the gate. Sitting upside down on a high platform were King Updownius The One Before Last and his wife Queen Updownia, while down at their hands sat Princess Updownina.

'"Your Royal Upsidedownity, Father of the Nation, just look at this absurdity and assess the situation,' said the

upside-down guard, pointing at me with his right foot.

'When the queen caught a glimpse of me, she let out a royal little squeal: "Oh my! A freak, and before noon! Shall I shriek, or shall I swoon?"

'A servant hurried over to the queen and footed her a glass of water.

'All the king's advisors and ministers looked at me, shocked. They mumbled, "It's inconceivable, unbelievable! Such a thing is unachievable. It's twisted; it's perverse! Have our enemies sent us a curse?"

'"Your name, pitiful sir, I command, and how you came to our glorious land," the king asked me.

'"I am Uncle Leo and I am on a journey through the Romanian steppes. I arrived here by chance."

'"King Topsy-Turvy Crown, Great Foot of Upsidown," said one of the advisors to the king, "allow me to comment on what we are seeing and warn you right now about the strange being. If you don't make this an utmost priority, it's bound to reverse your royal authority."

'"Your Majesty, my sire, safeguard your throne," said another advisor, "lest this intruder upend all we've ever known."

'A third advisor joined in, "This insult to our way of

life will surely lead to ruin and strife."

'And then one of the oldest advisors got to his hands and said in a trembling voice, "I predict a financial recession. Foot-walking will become a public obsession. Dozens of families will demand compensation, thereby capsizing our down-minded nation."

'All the ministers and advisors nodded their heads.

'"Excuse me, Your Majesty," said I. "Where I come from, everyone walks on their feet!"

'"What?!" cried everyone in the room.

'"It cannot be true!" gasped the queen. "It's a social taboo! Walking on their feet—what a pose! That's worse than eating with their hideous toes!"

'Only the upside-down Princess Updownina kept quiet and said not a word.

'Then King Updownius The One Before Last raised his sceptre and announced, "The problem must be handled now and today, and Upsidown saved from going astray. A solution is afoot; here's our royal plan: we shall have a nice stoning to destroy the wrong-way man."

'"Stoning? People will throw rocks at me?" I asked, trembling with fright.

'"Yes. Stoning," answered King Updownius.

'Two upside-down soldiers walking on either side of me took me to a prison cell. I sat in jail and tried to think of a way out. I didn't know how to escape the death sentence I had been given by King Updownius The One Before Last. I thought and thought, but I couldn't find any way around the strange punishment. I was very sad.

'The next morning, the two soldiers took me to the city square. They stood me against a wall, and all the people of the kingdom stood across from me on their hands, holding stones in their feet. The strong men and the big women held large rocks, the children and old people held medium-sized rocks, and the toddlers held little pebbles. All of them were aiming their stones at me. I knew the end was near. The king sat there on his

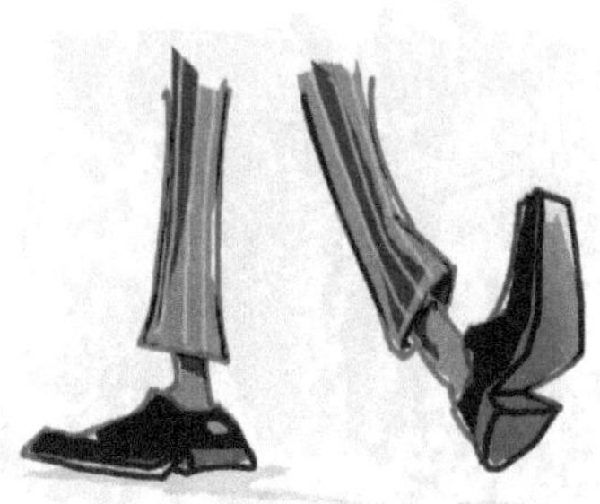

throne, with Queen Updownia beside him and Princess Updownina down at their hands. The king raised a foot and all his subjects quietened down.

'King Updownius The One Before Last turned to me and asked, "Before we start the stoning celebration, do you have a request or lamentation?"

'I hadn't any clue what to say, but then I got a sudden idea.

'"Yes, I do have one request."

'"What is it?" asked the king.

'"To dance."

'"Dance? What is dance?" asked the king. The people whispered, "Dance? What is dance, for goodness' sake? There's no such thing; it's a trick and a fake."

'"If you release me, I'll show you," I said.

'But one of the advisors rushed to say, "Unchaining

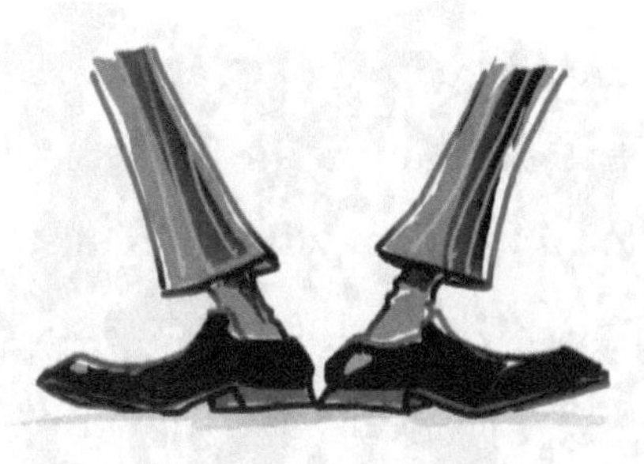

this creature and letting him loose would be asking for trouble and long-term abuse!"

'King Updownius The One Before Last said, "That would be a sin, so let the stoning begin!"

'Then Princess Updownina piped up, crying, "No, wait! I think we should give the convict a chance to show us what he means by asking to 'dance'!"

'In response to the princess' request, King Updownius The One Before Last signalled with his feet and the two soldiers released me. I took a few steps forward and then started to dance. I danced right and I danced left. I jumped with my feet tucked up in the air and then out to the sides. I twirled around on them. I tap danced with them. I did the pasodoble, the cha-cha-cha, the Charleston. I waltzed, I tangoed, I danced the hip hop, the salsa, the samba. I pirouetted through the air. I did the splits. I danced like I had never danced before.

'I finished dancing and stood panting in front of the crowd. There was silence for a moment, and then all the people burst out in laughter. The king, the queen and all the advisors joined in. Even Princess Updownina laughed. They all laughed, waving their feet around enthusiastically. I resumed dancing.

'The king lifted his feet again, the people quietened down and I stopped dancing. The princess stood on her hands and said, "Dear father, never have I seen such a pretty delight. This man could make our gloomy days bright. The death sentence should be taken back and he should give court jesting a crack."

'No one said a word. Everyone waited for the king to speak. He stretched out a foot and announced, "Ruling a kingdom can be totally dreary, and what you just did was ever so cheery. A little entertainment indeed fits the bill. Each morning and night you'll show off your skill. Rather than stoning, we've found better sport: we hereby appoint you Jester of Court."

'I was incredibly happy that my life had been spared. All the people laid their rocks down and went off to their homes. I went to live in the palace, and twice a day, I performed for King Updownius The One Before Last, Queen Updownia and Princess Updownina.

'And that's how I became the court jester of the Kingdom of Upsidown,' said Uncle Leo.

The story amused me very much.

'Do everything you tell me really happen?' I asked Uncle Leo.

'Of course it does; it's as true as can be,' said Uncle Leo.

'So why doesn't Graham believe it, and why does he say that stories are just chopped baloney?' I asked.

'I have an idea,' said Uncle Leo. 'Ask Graham to join us next week when I come for a visit.'

'Okay,' I agreed.

In the evening Mom, Dad, Graham and I were eating dinner. We had scrambled eggs and salad. Graham picked up some bits of egg and put them on a slice of bread.

'Graham, don't eat with your fingers. That's really barbaric,' said Mom.

'But Mom,' I said, 'did you know that in the Kingdom

of Upsidown you aren't supposed to eat with your toes?'

'Upsidown?' asked Mom.

'Yes. Uncle Leo told me today about the Kingdom of Upsidown.'

'So what did he tell you this time?' asked Graham.

'That in the Kingdom of Upsidown they walk on their hands and hold their forks with their toes,' I answered.

'So they are allowed to eat with their feet?' joked Graham.

'No, but Uncle Leo himself ate with his fingers today. There are places where they eat with their fingers and others where they eat with sticks.'

'Really?' asked Graham.

'Yes. And he also invited you specially to hear the story he's going to tell next Wednesday,' I told Graham.

'That's great!' said Graham. 'So I can eat with my fingers too, like Uncle Leo, can't I?' he asked Mom.

'Only if I stand on my head like in the Kingdom of Upsidown,' said Mom, and Graham and I burst out laughing.

Uncle Leo and the Story-swallowing Demon

On the following Wednesday, Uncle Leo came to visit us as usual. Graham and I were waiting for him on the balcony. He sat down on the armchair and said, 'It's so nice you came, Graham. Today I am going to tell you a special story, about the story-swallowing demon.'

Uncle Leo leaned back in his chair and began: 'One day the Chief of Police of the Romanian steppes called me. He told me, "Uncle Leo, we have a serious problem, a terrible problem; we are in big trouble! There's a demon going through every single city and village in the country and swallowing up all stories. You must help us catch him." The Chief of Police started crying, "I just don't know what to do!"

'I immediately went over to the police station, where I heard all about the story-swallowing demon.

'The demon simply liked eating stories. He ate children's stories and grownups' stories, long stories and short stories. This demon swallowed all the letters in all the stories in all the books. When mothers wanted to read a story to their children, they would open the book and find empty pages.

'The demon also swallowed stories that people tell. For example, if a boy came home from school and his mother asked him, "What did you do at school today?", as soon as the boy started telling his mother what had happened at school, the demon would show up and swallow the story, leaving the child with nothing to tell.

'Or for instance, if that same boy's father came home late at night and the boy's mother asked him, "Where have you been? Why didn't you call? I was worried about you!", as soon as the father started to tell her all sorts of stories that would explain why he had come back so late, the story-swallowing demon would come and swallow up the father's stories, and the mother wouldn't know what had actually happened.

'All the favorite stories disappeared from the kingdom: Winnie-the-Pooh, Snow White, Sleeping Beauty, Little Red Riding Hood, The Little Engine That Could and Goodnight Moon—the demon swallowed them all. It became worse at night, when the story-swallowing demon swallowed people's dreams, because dreams are the stories that people see at night. People slept, but didn't dream anything. And the demon swallowed up all the memories people keep in their heads, too.

'The situation was just awful. The Romanian Steppes Police Force had announced a state of emergency, which was why the Chief of Police had summoned me.

'"Don't worry," I told the Chief of Police. "I will get the stories back to the people. Just tell me where this demon hides."

'"According to the reports we have received," said the Chief of Police, "he hides in a dark cave in the far north."

'I immediately set out for the far north. I took supplies with me for the way: a map, hiking boots, a hat, and a pickle, in case I got hungry. I marched to the far north. I walked and walked until I saw the opening of a huge, dark cave. I climbed up to the entrance but before going into the cave, I listened.'

'What did you hear?' I asked Uncle Leo.

'I heard "Minyum-yum-yum, shinyum-yum-yum"—that was the sound of the demon swallowing stories. I knew that the demon was now eating a story for lunch. Before going into the cave, I turned myself invisible so the demon wouldn't be able to catch me.'

'How did you make yourself invisible?' asked Graham.

'I have a way,' said Uncle Leo, but he didn't tell us what it was. He continued with his story: 'I entered carefully. At first I couldn't see anything because it was so dark, but slowly my eyes got used to the darkness and I managed to see the demon. The story-swallowing demon was sitting on a rock and eating a long, long, long story.

After he finished the long story, he had a short children's story in rhyme for dessert. Then he stretched out on the ground.

'"Hey! Story-swallowing demon!" I called out to him.

'"Who's that?" he growled. "Who dares to disturb my afternoon nap?"

'"I didn't come here to bother you," I said. "I came to visit you."

'The demon looked all around, but he couldn't see me because I was invisible. He was confused. "What do you mean, 'You came to visit me'? How is that possible? Everyone's afraid of me!" he exclaimed.

'"I don't see what there is to be afraid of," I said.

'"I eat up everyone's stories," said the demon.

'"Good! Great! I came to tell you an especially delicious story," I said.

'"Really?"

'"That's right."

'"But I already had lunch," said the demon.

'"Don't worry about that," I said. "Stories give you an appetite."'

'What story did you tell him?' asked my brother Graham, looking concerned.

'First I told him how I got stuck on a cloud. Then I told him how my four hairs saved my life. But this demon was a glutton. He enjoyed the stories, but when I had finished he just said, "More! I want more stories!" So I told him how I had once turned into a cockroach. I also told him how I became the court jester in the Kingdom of Upsidown.'

'And what did he do?' I asked.

'He immediately swallowed all the stories. I thought that eventually he would get full and fall asleep, but after each story he said, "More! I want more stories!"

'I didn't know what to do. I was afraid this demon would gobble up all my stories. But then I had an idea. I started telling him about a boy who was bored, bored, bored. This boy was really bored. He didn't feel like doing anything and just sat, bored, bored, bored. Just sat and sat...and I kept telling the demon this long, boring, boring, boring, boring story. The story was so boring that the story-swallowing demon simply fell asleep. He lay down on the ground and snored.

'I immediately went over to him, opened his mouth and took all the stories he had swallowed out of his stomach. I set the stories loose outside, and they all went back to their rightful places: the written stories flew back into the books, the stories people had told returned to their mouths, dreams went back to sleep, and memories went back to heads.'

'But what happened when the demon woke up?' asked my brother Graham.

'Ah, now, that was a very big problem,' answered Uncle Leo. 'The demon woke up raging and storming. He screamed, "What is this? Who stole all the stories from my stomach? I'm hungry! I have to eat a story immediately! I'm *starving!* My belly is empty! Who had the nerve to steal my stories? Get over here! Show your face!" He was raging, but I was invisible.

'I called out to him, "Wait! I'll tell you a story! Don't worry! I'll tell you a really delicious story!"

'"Tell me, tell me!" yelled the demon.'

'What did you tell him?' I asked Uncle Leo.

'I told him *his* story: I told him about the story-

swallowing demon that swallowed everybody's stories. I told him how he had swallowed up the stories written in books, stories from people's mouths, and all the dreams. The demon heard this story and eagerly swallowed it. Since the story I was telling him was about him, he also swallowed himself up, and disappeared. And that's how the Romanian steppes were saved from the story-swallowing demon,' said Uncle Leo.

I looked at my brother Graham.

'That story was a lot of fun,' said Graham. 'But you don't really know how to make yourself invisible, do you?'

'Actually, I do,' said Uncle Leo.

'Could you do it right now?' I asked him.

'It's been a long time since I turned invisible, but I can try. I just need you to help me. Close your eyes and count to three.'

Graham and I closed our eyes, counted 'One, two, three,' and then opened our eyes.

'Where's Uncle Leo?' Graham asked. 'Where's he disappeared to?' I asked.

Uncle Leo really had disappeared! He wasn't on the balcony and we couldn't find him anywhere in the entire house.

'Now do you see that Uncle Leo's stories are real?' I asked my brother Graham.

He had no choice and simply said, 'Yeah, I guess they're real.'

'And not just real. They're also the best stories in the world,' I said.

'That's true,' said Graham.

And then we heard Dad calling us. 'Come to dinner!' We went to the kitchen and ate dinner together—Dad, Mom, Graham and me.

Today is Wednesday. Graham and I know that Uncle Leo will come visit us again today and tell us one of his adventures—maybe a happy one, maybe a sad one, maybe a scary one and maybe a funny one. Graham and I don't argue any more over whether Uncle Leo's adventures are real or not, because Uncle Leo has so many stories, and we love to listen to them as much as we love ice cream or chocolate. Maybe even more.

www.ingramcontent.com/pod-product-compliance
Lightning Source LLC
Chambersburg PA
CBHW030336310726
48979CB00001B/61

* 9 7 8 8 1 2 9 1 3 4 6 3 9 *